YIKES, IT'S A YETI!

Karen Wallace

Illustrated by Mick Reid

Hi!
I'm Norman's
granny.
Come with us
and hunt
a yeti!

comix

First paperback edition 2001
First published 2001 in hardback by
A & C Black (Publishers) Ltd
37 Soho Square, London, W1D 3QZ

ISBN 0-7136-5842-8

A CIP catalogue for this book is available from the
British Library.

Printed and bound in Spain by G. Z. Printek, Bilbao

CHAPTER ONE

Norman Nomates lived with his mum and dad at Number 22 Ditchwater Drive. It was a nice little house on a nice little road.

Every day Norman went to school. Every day he came home from school.

Except on the weekends and the holidays.

That's when no one goes to school!

Nothing exciting ever happened to Norman.

His collection of fishing gnomes never caught any fish.

His collection of snails never escaped from their box.

We like it here.

Poor Norman!
Exciting things happened to other people.
And they always happened to Slick Sid.

Slick Sid was Norman's next-door neighbour and they were in the same class at school.

Every day something exciting happened to Slick Sid. According to Slick Sid, that is.

Slick Sid had always made Norman feel really boring. Even when they were babies.

Norman's mum tried everything to make things more exciting for Norman. Once she put a rose in her mouth and told him he was half Spanish.

Norman was stunned. He really liked the idea of having a foreign name. At last something exciting had happened! At last there was something he could tell his friends.

I'm half Spanish, you know. My real name's Norman NOMATEZ.

But Norman's dad wasn't having any of it.

Get down off the table, Doris.

No more Spanish evening-classes for you!

So Norman's mum went back to arranging dried flowers and Norman went back to his fishing gnomes and his snails. And after that, no one mentioned NOMATEZ again.

CHAPTER TWO

It seemed to Norman that Sid Slick always had the coolest shoes, the greatest T-shirt and the shiniest jacket. Slick Sid even knew how to lean against a bicycle so that he looked like a racing star.

Now, if Norman had cool shoes, somehow he would have stepped in a puddle.

If Norman had the greatest T-shirt and the same shiny jacket, somehow his mum would have shrunk them in the wash.

And as for leaning against a bicycle...

Forget it!

One day Norman was hunting for snails in the garden. Norman really liked snails. He had all kinds in his collection. Big ones, little ones, stripy ones and spotty ones.

Norman had just discovered a huge black snail when his mum rushed out of the door.

Something exciting, Norman!

Norman looked up. His heart banged in his chest!

What?

Your granny is coming to take you camping!

Norman wished with all his heart that he could turn into a snail. His mum might as well have driven down Ditchwater Drive shouting through a megaphone.

Extra! Extra! Read All About it!
Norman Nomates Goes on Really Uncool Camping Trip with his Granny!

Because even though Norman really liked his granny, it just wasn't cool to go camping with her.

Norman crouched down and tried to make himself as small as possible. He tried to edge sideways and hide under a bush.

Too late!

All the boys and girls on Ditchwater Drive raced into Norman's garden. Slick Sid got there first.

Pimply Pete pulled a face.

Stringy Alice and Big-Eared Eric and Doughhead Dave all had a different idea.

There was a POOP! POOP! A little grey car spluttered to a stop outside Norman's front gate.

A little grey-haired old lady climbed out.

She wore a dress with roses on it and a small round hat.

Cooee! Norman!

Poor Norman! All his friends fell about giggling.
Slick Sid was laughing so hard he could hardly
speak.

He threw back his head and hooted.

Norman's mum handed him a suitcase.

Norman didn't want her to embarrass him any more. He wished the ground would open and swallow him up! But of course it didn't because that sort of thing only happens in films.

Norman's granny started up the little grey car. Norman looked out at Stringy Alice, Big-Eared Eric and Doughhead Dave. They were jumping up and down and waving.

Beside them Pimply Pete and Slick Sid were doing handstands and waggling their feet in the air. Norman said nothing and looked down at his hands. Even his fingers were blushing!

CHAPTER THREE

Then something extraordinary happened! As soon as the little grey car had gone round the corner, Norman's granny pulled over and jumped out.

She took off her dress, she ripped off her little round hat. And she yanked off her curly grey hair.

Norman couldn't believe his eyes! His granny had a brilliant brush-cut.

And she was wearing a leather combat suit!

Norman's mouth dropped open. He didn't know what to say. Norman's granny punched him playfully on the arm.

It was a long way to the Himalayas.

First they took a great big plane and flew over the sea.

Then they took a medium-sized plane and flew over the mountains.

Then they took a really tiny plane and dived in and out of the clouds.

Norman thought of Slick Sid and a big smile spread across his face.

This beats a motorbike any day!

It was sunset (in the foothills of the Himalayas, of course). Norman and his granny walked into a little village.

At first all the houses seemed empty.
And there wasn't a single pizza parlour, hamburger joint or a greasy spoon café anywhere.

Norman didn't want to say anything, but it was well past his supper time.

Not long now!

Granny raised her eyebrows.

I hope you're feeling hungry.

Norman was puzzled.

Is someone expecting us for supper?

For supper?

Goodness me, no! We're going to a FEAST!

Suddenly a thousand fireworks burst into the air. Lights came on in every window and a huge cheer went up. A stocky little man wearing a huge sheepskin coat ran down the street.

Greetings, Glorious Granny!

Welcome back!

Greetings, Grabtucker.

Is the Feast hot and greasy?

Norman watched in amazement as they did a kind of high-five handshake and danced from foot to foot.

The way you like it, Glorious One!

Excellent! My grandson is hungry!

31

Five minutes later Norman was munching a yak burger and gulping down a large yak milkshake. It was the most delicious supper he had ever eaten. There was just one thing missing.

Grabtucker banged a bottle of ketchup on the table. Norman's eyes went round as saucers.

How did you know?

Your Glorious Granny told us.

He lifted his arm.

You can't have burgers without ketchup!

The next day Granny took Norman outside and pointed to a huge mountain covered in snow.

That's pretty.

That's where we're going.

An extraordinary thought occurred to Norman.

Do you come here often?

CHAPTER FOUR

Norman remembered what he used to think grannies did on holiday.

Grannies went on cruises.

How many seagulls have you counted, dear?

Grannies played cards and drank tea.

I'll raise you a lump. One card or two, dear?

Grannies walked little dogs and sat on park benches.

Here comes lunch!

Grannies played golf when it was sunny.

This walking is hard work.

Grannies visited gardens and looked at flowers.

I've got a rose like that.

Norman thought about what he knew his granny did on holiday now.

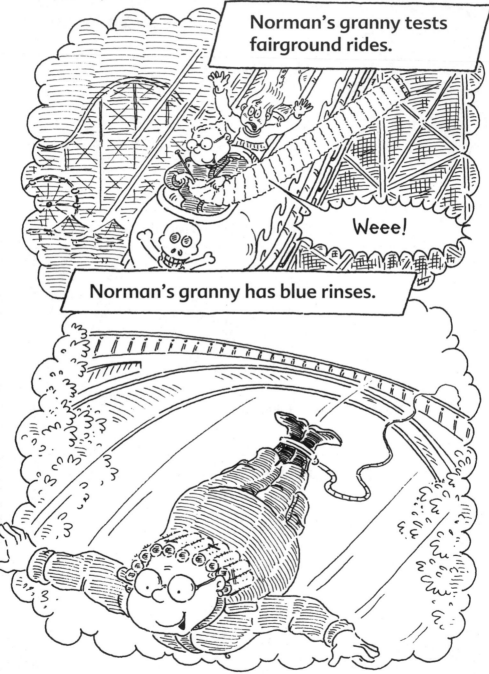

Norman's granny tests fairground rides.

Weee!

Norman's granny has blue rinses.

That afternoon Norman drove a sledge pulled by six big wolves.

It's easier than riding a bicycle.

That's what he thinks.

He swung over a ravine on a rope bridge. He put on a pair of snow shoes and followed his granny half way up the huge mountain.

After a supper of yak burgers and yakshake (it was just as good as the first time), Granny pulled a large picture out of her bag.

This is why we're here.

We're going to find the yeti.

Norman couldn't believe his ears.

But yetis don't exist.

Oh yes they do.

She gave him a cunning look.

I found their footprints last year.

That night Norman couldn't get to sleep for ages. So many exciting things had happened to him, he thought he might explode!

A warm, happy feeling spread up through his knees.

Wait till I tell Slick Sid!

Yikes! It's a yeti!

Norman jumped out of his sleeping bag! A strange hairy thing was standing over him!

Good morning, dear.

The hairy thing's hand pulled off the hairy thing's head! It wasn't a yeti. It was Norman's granny in a yeti suit!

Five minutes later, Norman looked like a yeti, too.

She zipped up the back of Norman's suit.

She did up Norman's top button.

Norman stared at the yeti face mask.

Norman's granny packed a picnic of...

Yak burgers and yakshake.

And held up a very large, old-fashioned camera.

We have to take a picture.

The world must know of our discovery!

Norman stared at the camera. It had a huge silvery flash bulb. It was the kind that went BANG! when you pressed the button. A nasty nervous feeling fluttered in Norman's stomach. What if the yetis didn't want their picture taken?

ANYTHING COULD HAPPEN!

CHAPTER FIVE

All that morning Norman and his granny looked for yeti footprints.

They investigated trees.

Yetis love swinging.

They paddled in streams.

Yetis love swimming.

They looked around rock piles. Norman's granny seemed nervous.

Throwing boulders is one of their favourite games.

At last Norman's granny found some footprints. But they were in the middle of nowhere! They were deep and wide with six long toes.

Norman's granny pointed to a cliff.

It didn't take long to follow the tracks. They started by a tree branch. They stopped by a stream. They went round and round a rock pile. Norman and his granny exchanged looks. Huge boulders lay all over the place.

50

Even though Norman knew it was polite to let ladies go first, most times he forgot. But as he stood with his granny outside the mouth of an enormous dark cave, Norman got a severe attack of good manners.

After you, Granny.

Why, thank you, dear.

How terribly polite.

Norman and his granny crept into the cave. It was deep and dark and unbelievably smelly. Norman looked at the floor and his stomach turned over. There were bones everywhere. And Norman knew that vegetables don't have bones.

That's no cabbage!

Suddenly they saw firelight glowing around a corner. Norman's granny turned to Norman and put her finger to her lips. Without a word, she passed him the camera.

They held their breath and crept up to the orange light.

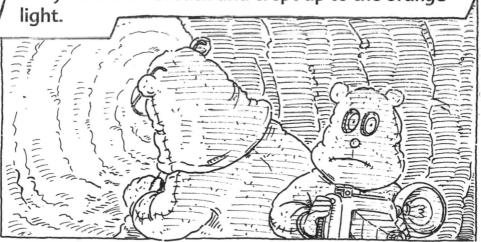

Suddenly three things happened.

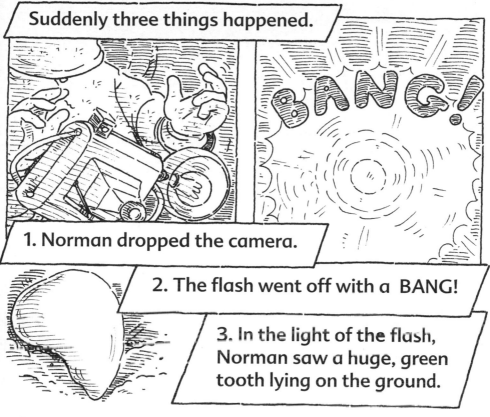

1. Norman dropped the camera.

2. The flash went off with a BANG!

3. In the light of the flash, Norman saw a huge, green tooth lying on the ground.

Then the ground began to shudder as enormous feet thundered towards them.

Norman stuffed the green tooth in his pocket and they ran as fast as they could.

Luckily, the yeti was tired out from swinging, swimming and throwing rocks. He didn't want to play chase. (Besides, he had another camera to add to his collection.)

That night Grabtucker put on a wonderful feast.

FAREWELL TO GLORIOUS GRANNY
AND HER GRANDSON NORMAN

Guess what they ate?

CHAPTER SIX

It was a long way back to 22 Ditchwater Drive.

First they took a tiny plane.

Then they took a steam train.

Then they took a really big plane that flew over the mountains and the sea.

It was almost tea-time when the little grey car spluttered up to 22 Ditchwater Drive.

Pimply Pete and Stringy Alice and Big-Eared Eric and Doughhead Dave were waiting. There was no sign of Slick Sid anywhere.

Norman told them the whole story.

Pimply Pete was gobsmacked. Stringy Alice was stunned. Doughhead David was amazed. Even Big-Eared Eric couldn't believe his ears.

That's when Norman reached into his pocket and pulled out...
a huge, dirty, green tooth!

And everyone stopped laughing right away!

At that moment Slick Sid showed up. He was covered in bandages and hobbling on crutches.

For the first time in his life, Norman didn't feel boring, he actually felt sorry for Slick Sid. He even thought that they could be real friends.

Norman grinned and patted Slick Sid on the shoulder.